"Wow," whispered Jack. "I wish I could see a Pteranodon for real."

Jack studied the picture of the odd-looking creature soaring through the sky.

"Arghh!" screamed Annie.

"What?" said Jack.

"A monster!" Annie cried. She pointed to the tree-house window.

"Stop pretending, Annie," said Jack.

"No, really!" said Annie.

Jack looked out of the window.

A giant creature was gliding above the treetops! He had a long, weird crest on the back of his head. A skinny beak. And huge bat-like wings!

It was a real live Pteranodon!

Read all the adventures of
Jack and **Annie**!

1–4: The Mystery of the Tree House

5–8: The Mystery of the Magic Spell

9–12: The Mystery of the Ancient Riddles

Coming soon:

Magic Tree House

VALLEY of the DINOSAURS

MARY POPE OSBORNE

Illustrated by Philippe Masson

RED FOX

VALLEY OF THE DINOSAURS
A RED FOX BOOK 978 1 862 30523 6

First published in Great Britain by Red Fox,
an imprint of Random House Children's Books
A Random House Group Company

Published in the US by Random House Children's Books,
a division of Random House Inc, 1992

Red Fox edition published 2008

9 10 8

The Random House Group Limited supports The Forest Stewardship Council
(FSC), the leading international forest certification organisation. All our titles
that are printed on Greenpeace approved FSC certified paper carry the FSC
logo. Our paper procurement policy can be found at:
www.rbooks.co.uk/environment

Mixed Sources
Product group from well-managed
forests and other controlled sources
www.fsc.org Cert no. TT-COC-2139
© 1996 Forest Stewardship Council

Set in Bembo Schoolbook

Red Fox Books are published by Random House Children's Books,
61–63 Uxbridge Road, London W5 5SA

www.**kids**at**randomhouse**.co.uk
www.**rbooks**.co.uk

Addresses for companies within The Random House Group Limited can be found at:
www.randomhouse.co.uk/offices.htm

THE RANDOM HOUSE GROUP Limited Reg. No. 954009

A CIP catalogue record for this book is available from the British Library.

Printed in the UK by CPI Bookmarque, Croydon, CR0 4TD

For Linda and Mallory,
who took the trip with me

Contents

1

Into the Woods

"Help! A monster!" said Annie.

"Yes, sure," said Jack. "A real monster in Frog Valley."

"Run, Jack!" said Annie. She ran up the road.

Great!

This is what he got for spending time with his seven-year-old sister.

Annie loved pretend stuff. But Jack was eight and a half. He liked *real* things.

"Watch out, Jack! The monster's coming! Race you!"

"No, thanks," said Jack.

Annie raced alone into the woods.

Jack looked at the sky. The sun was about to set.

"Come on, Annie! It's time to go home!"

But Annie had disappeared.

Jack waited.

No Annie.

"Annie!" he shouted again.

"Jack! Jack! Come here!"

Jack groaned. "This better be good," he said.

Jack left the road and headed into the woods. The trees were lit with golden late-afternoon light.

"Come here!" called Annie.

There she was. Standing under a tall oak tree. "Look," she said. She was pointing at a rope ladder.

The longest rope ladder Jack had ever seen.

"Wow," he whispered.

The ladder went all the way up to the top of the tree.

There — at the top — was a tree house. It was tucked between two branches.

"That must be the highest tree house in the world," said Annie.

"Who built it?" asked Jack. "I've never seen it before."

"I don't know. But I'm going up," said Annie.

"No. We don't know who it belongs to," said Jack.

"Just for a teeny minute," said Annie. She started up the ladder.

"Annie, come back!"

She kept climbing.

Jack sighed. "Annie, it's almost dark. We have to go home."

Annie disappeared inside the tree house.

"An-nie!"

Jack waited a moment. He was about to call again when Annie poked her head out of the tree-house window.

"Books!" she shouted.

"What?"

"It's filled with books!"

Oh, wow! Jack loved books.

He pushed his glasses into place. He gripped the sides of the rope ladder, and up he went.

2

The Monster

Jack crawled through a hole in the tree-house floor.

Wow. The tree house *was* filled with books. Books everywhere. Very old books with dusty covers. New books with shiny, bright covers.

"Look. You can see far, far away," said Annie. She was peering out of the tree-house window.

Jack looked out of the window with her. Down below were the tops of the other trees. In the distance he saw the

Frog Valley library.

The primary school. The park.

Annie pointed in the other direction.

"There's our house," she said.

Sure enough, there was their house.

Next door was their neighbour's black

dog, Henry. He looked very tiny.

"Hi, Henry!" shouted Annie.

"Shhh!" said Jack. "We're not supposed

to be up here."

He glanced around the tree house again.

"I wonder who owns all these books," he said. He noticed bookmarks were sticking out of many of them.

"I like this one," said Annie. She held up a book with a castle on the cover.

"Here's a book about Frog Valley," said Jack. He turned to the page with the bookmark.

"Hey, there's a picture of *these* woods in here," said Jack.

"Oh, here's a book for you," said Annie. She held up a book about dinosaurs.

"Let me see it." Jack grabbed the book from her.

"You look at that one, and I'll look at the one about castles," said Annie.

"No, we better not," said Jack. "We don't know who these books belong to."

But even as he said this, Jack opened the dinosaur book to where the bookmark was. He couldn't help himself.

He turned to a picture of an ancient flying reptile. A Pteranodon.

He touched the huge bat-like wings.

"Wow," whispered Jack. "I wish I could see a Pteranodon for real."

Jack studied the picture of the odd-looking creature soaring through the sky.

"Ahhh!" screamed Annie.

"What?" said Jack.

"A monster!" Annie cried. She pointed to the tree-house window.

"Stop pretending, Annie," said Jack.

"No, really!" said Annie.

Jack looked out of the window.

A giant creature was gliding above the treetops! He had a long, weird crest on the back of his head. A skinny beak. And huge bat-like wings!

It was a real live Pteranodon!

The creature curved through the sky.

He was coming straight towards the tree house. He looked like a glider plane!

The wind began to blow.

The leaves trembled.

Suddenly the creature soared up. High into the sky. Jack nearly fell out of the window trying to see him.

The wind picked up. It was whistling now.

The tree house started to spin.

"What's happening?" cried Jack.

"Get down!" shouted Annie.

She pulled him away from the window.

The tree house was spinning. Faster and faster.

Jack squeezed his eyes shut. He held on to Annie.

Then everything was still.

Absolutely still.

Jack opened his eyes. Sunlight slanted through the window.

There was Annie. The books. His rucksack.

The tree house was still high up in an oak tree.

But it wasn't the *same* oak tree.

3

Where Is Here?

Jack looked out of the window.

He looked down at the picture in the book.

He looked back out of the window.

The world outside and the world in the picture – they were exactly the same.

The Pteranodon was soaring through the sky. The ground was covered with ferns and tall grass. There was a winding stream. A sloping hill. And volcanoes in the distance.

"Wh-where are we?" stammered
Jack.

The Pteranodon glided down to the
base of their tree. The creature coasted to
a stop. And stood very still.

"What happened to us?" said Annie.
She looked at Jack. He looked at her.

"I don't know," said Jack. "I was
looking at the picture in the book—"

"And you said, 'Wow, I wish I could see a Pteranodon for real,'" said Annie.

"Yes. And then we saw one. In the Frog Valley woods," said Jack.

"Yes. And then the wind got loud. And the tree house started spinning," said Annie.

"And we landed here," said Jack.

"And we landed here," said Annie.

"So that means . . ." said Jack.

"So that means . . . what?" said Annie.

"Nothing," said Jack. He shook his head. "None of this can be real."

Annie looked out of the window again. "But *he's* real," she said. "He's *very* real."

Jack looked out of the window with her. The Pteranodon was standing at the base of the oak tree. Like a guard. His giant wings were spread out on either side of him.

"Hi!" Annie shouted.

"Shhh!" said Jack. "We're not supposed to be here."

"But where is *here*?" said Annie.

"I don't know," said Jack.

"Hi!" Annie called again to the creature. The Pteranodon looked up at them.

"Where is *here*?" Annie called down.

"You're crazy. He can't talk," said Jack. "But maybe the book can tell us."

Jack looked down at the book. He read the words under the picture:

This flying reptile lived in the Cretaceous period. It vanished 65 million years ago.

No. Impossible. They couldn't have landed in a time sixty-five million years ago.

"Jack," said Annie. "He's nice."

"Nice?"

"Yes, I can tell. Let's go down and talk to him."

"Talk to him?"

Annie started down the rope ladder.

"Hey!" shouted Jack.

But Annie kept going.

"Are you crazy?" Jack called.

Annie dropped to the ground. She stepped boldly up to the ancient creature.

4
Henry

Jack gasped as Annie held out her hand.

Oh, no. She was always trying to make friends with animals. But this was going too far.

"Don't get too close to him, Annie!" Jack shouted.

But Annie touched the Pteranodon's crest. She stroked his neck. She was talking to him.

What in the world was she saying?

Jack took a deep breath. OK. He would go down too. It would be good to examine the creature. Take notes. Like a scientist.

Jack started down the rope ladder.

When he got to the ground, he was only a couple of metres away from the creature.

The creature stared at Jack. His eyes were bright and alert.

"He's soft, Jack," said Annie. "He feels like Henry."

Jack snorted. "He's no dog, Annie."

"Feel him, Jack," said Annie.

Jack didn't move.

"Don't think, Jack. Just do it."

Jack stepped forward. He put out his arm. Very cautiously. He brushed his hand down the creature's neck.

Interesting. A thin layer of fuzz covered the Pteranodon's skin.

"Soft, isn't it?" said Annie.

Jack reached into his rucksack and pulled out a pencil and a notebook. He wrote:

fuzzy skin

"What are you doing?" asked Annie.

"Taking notes," said Jack. "We're probably the first people in the whole world to ever see a real live Pteranodon."

Jack looked at the Pteranodon again. The creature had a bony crest on top of his head. The crest was longer than Jack's arm.

"I wonder how clever he is," Jack said.

"*Very* clever," said Annie.

"Don't count on it," said Jack. "His brain's probably no bigger than a bean."

"No, he's very clever. I can feel it," said Annie. "I'm going to call him Henry."

Jack wrote in his notebook:

small brain?

He looked at the creature again. "Maybe he's a mutant," he said.

The creature tilted his head.

Annie laughed. "He's not a mutant, Jack."

"Well, what's he doing here then? Where is this place?" said Jack.

Annie leaned close to the Pteranodon.

"Do you know where we are, Henry?" she asked softly.

The creature fixed his eyes on Annie. His long jaws were opening and closing. Like a giant pair of scissors.

"Are you trying to talk to me, Henry?" asked Annie.

"Forget it, Annie." Jack wrote in his

notebook:

mouth
like
scissors?

"Did we come
to a time long ago,
Henry?" asked
Annie. "Is this a
place from long
ago?" Suddenly she
gasped. "Jack!"
He looked up.
Annie was
pointing
towards the
hill. On top
stood a huge
dinosaur!

25

5

Gold in the Grass

"Go! *Go!*" said Jack. He threw his notebook into his bag. He pushed Annie towards the rope ladder.

"Bye, Henry!" she said.

"Go!" said Jack. He gave Annie a big push.

"Stop it!" she said. But she started up the ladder. Jack scrambled after her.

They tumbled into the tree house.

They were panting as they looked out of the window at the dinosaur.

He was standing on the hilltop. Eating flowers off a tree.

"Oh, wow," whispered Jack. "We are in a time long ago!"

The dinosaur looked like a huge rhinoceros. Only he had three horns instead of one. Two long ones above his eyes and one on his nose. He had a big shield-like thing behind his head.

"Triceratops!" said Jack.

"Does he eat people?" whispered Annie.

"I'll look it up." Jack grabbed the dinosaur book. He flipped through the pages.

"There!" he said. He pointed to a picture of a Triceratops. He read the caption:

The Triceratops lived in the late Cretaceous period. This plant-eating dinosaur weighed over 5,500 kilos.

Jack slammed the book shut. "Just plants. No meat."

"Let's go and see him," said Annie.

"Are you crazy?" said Jack.

"Don't you want to take notes about him?" asked Annie. "We're probably the first people in the whole world to ever see a real live Triceratops."

Jack sighed. She was right.

"Let's go," he said.

He shoved the dinosaur book into his bag. He slung it over his shoulder and started down the ladder.

On the way down, Jack stopped.

He called up to Annie, "Just promise you won't pet him."

"I promise."

"Promise you won't kiss him."

"I promise."

"Promise you won't talk to him."

"I promise."

"Promise you won't—"

"Go! Go!" she said.

Jack went.

Annie followed.

When they stepped off the ladder, the Pteranodon gave them a kind look.

Annie blew a kiss at him. "Be back soon, Henry," she said cheerfully.

"Shhh!" said Jack. And he led the way through the ferns. Slowly and carefully.

When he reached the bottom of the hill, he knelt behind a fat bush.

Annie knelt beside him and started to speak.

"Shhh!" Jack put his finger to his lips.

Annie made a face.

Jack peeked out at the Triceratops.

The dinosaur was incredibly big. Bigger than a truck. He was eating the flowers off a magnolia tree.

Jack slipped his notebook out of his pack. He wrote:

eats flowers

Annie nudged him.

Jack ignored her. He studied the
Triceratops again. He wrote:

eats slowly

Annie nudged him hard.

Jack looked at her.

Annie pointed to herself. She walked
her fingers through the air. She pointed
to the dinosaur. She smiled.

Was she teasing?

She waved at Jack.

Jack started to grab her.

She laughed and jumped away. She fell
into the grass. In full view of the
Triceratops!

"Get back!" whispered Jack.

Too late. The big dinosaur had spotted
Annie. He gazed down at her from the
hilltop. Half a magnolia flower was

sticking out of his mouth.

"Oops," said Annie.

"Get back!" Jack shouted at her.

"He looks nice, Jack."

"Nice? Watch out for his horns, Annie!"

"No. He's nice, Jack."

Nice?

But the Triceratops just gazed calmly down at Annie. Then he turned and loped away. Down the side of the hill.

"Bye!" said Annie. She turned back to
Jack. "See?"

Jack grunted. But he wrote in his
notebook:

nice

"Come on. Let's look around some
more," said Annie.

As Jack started
after Annie, he
saw something
glittering in
the tall grass.
He reached
out and picked
it up.

A medallion.
A gold medallion.

A letter was engraved
on the medallion. A fancy M.

"Wow! Someone came here before us,"
Jack said softly.

6

Dinosaur Valley

"Annie, look at this!" Jack called. "Look what I found!"

Annie had gone up to the hilltop.

She was busy picking a flower from the magnolia tree.

"Annie, look! A medallion!"

But Annie wasn't paying attention to Jack. She was staring at something on the other side of the hill.

"Oh, wow!" she said.

"Annie!"

Clutching her magnolia flower, she set

off down the hill.

"Annie, come back!" Jack shouted.

But Annie had disappeared.

"I'm going to kill her," Jack muttered.

He stuffed the gold medallion into his jeans pocket.

Then he heard Annie shriek.

"Annie?"

Jack heard another sound as well. A deep, bellowing sound. Like a tuba.

"Jack! Come here!" Annie called.

"Annie!"

Jack grabbed his rucksack and raced
up the hill.

When he got to the top, he gasped.

The valley below was filled with nests.
Big nests made out of mud. And the nests
were filled with tiny dinosaurs!

Annie was crouching next to one of
the nests. And standing over her was a

gigantic duck-billed dinosaur!

"Don't panic. Don't move," said Jack.
He stepped slowly down the hill towards
Annie.

The huge dinosaur was towering
above Annie. Waving her arms. Making
her tuba sound.

Jack stopped. He didn't want to get too
close.

He knelt on the ground. "OK. Move
towards me. Slowly," he said.

Annie started to stand up.

"Don't stand. Crawl,"
said Jack.

Clutching her flower, Annie crawled towards Jack.

The duck-billed dinosaur followed her. Still bellowing.

Annie froze.

"Keep going," Jack said softly.

Annie started crawling again.

Jack inched further down the hill.

Until he was just an arm's distance from Annie.

He reached out – and grabbed her hand.

He pulled Annie towards him.

"Stay down," he said. He crouched next to her. "Bow your head. Pretend to chew."

"Chew?"

"Yes. I read that's what you do if a fierce dog comes at you."

"She's not a dog, Jack," said Annie.

"Just chew," said Jack.

Jack and Annie both bowed their heads. And pretended to chew.

Soon the dinosaur grew quiet.

Jack raised his head.

"I don't think she's cross any more," he said.

"Thanks, Jack, for saving me," said Annie.

"You have to use your brain," said Jack. "You can't just go running up to a nest of babies. There's always a mother nearby."

Annie stood up.

"Annie!"

Too late.

Annie held out her magnolia flower to the dinosaur.

"I'm sorry I made you worry about your babies," she said.

The dinosaur moved closer to Annie. She grabbed the flower from her. She reached for another.

"No more," said Annie.

The dinosaur let out a sad tuba sound.

"But there are more flowers up there," Annie said. She pointed to the top of the hill. "I'll get you some."

Annie hurried up the hill.

The dinosaur waddled after her.

Jack quickly examined the babies. Some were crawling out of their nests.

Where were the other mothers?

Jack took out the dinosaur book. He flipped through the pages.

He found a picture of some duck-billed dinosaurs. He read the caption:

The Anatosauruses lived in colonies. While a few mothers baby-sat the nests, others hunted for food.

So there must be more mothers close by.

"Hey, Jack!" Annie called.

Jack looked up. Annie was at the top of the hill. Feeding magnolia flowers to the giant Anatosaurus!

"She's nice, too, Jack," Annie said.

But suddenly the Anatosaurus made

her terrible tuba sound. Annie crouched down and started to chew.

The dinosaur barged down the hill.

She seemed afraid of something.

Jack put the book down on top of his bag. He hurried up to Annie.

"I wonder why she ran away," said Annie. "We were starting to be friends."

Jack looked around. What he saw in the distance almost made him faint.

An enormous ugly monster was coming across the plain.

He was walking on two big legs. And swinging a long, thick tail. And dangling two tiny arms.

He had a huge head. And his jaws were wide open.

Even from far away Jack could see his long, gleaming teeth.

"Tyrannosaurus rex!" he whispered.

7

Ready, Steady, Go!

"Run, Annie! Run!" cried Jack. "To the tree house!"

They dashed down the hill together. Through the tall grass, through the ferns, past the Pteranodon, and across to the rope ladder.

They scrambled up. Seconds later they tumbled into the tree house.

Annie leaped to the window.

"He's going away!" she said, panting.

Jack pushed his glasses into place. He looked through the window with her.

The Tyrannosaurus was wandering off.

But then the monster stopped and turned round.

"Duck!" said Jack.

The two of them crouched down.

After a long moment, they raised their heads. They peeped out again.

"Coast clear," said Jack.

"Yes!" whispered Annie.

"We have to get out of here," said Jack.

"You made a wish before," said Annie.

"I wish we could go back to Frog Valley," said Jack.

Nothing happened.

"I wish—"

"Wait. You were looking at a picture in the dinosaur book. Remember?"

The dinosaur book.

Jack groaned. "Oh, no. I left the book

and my bag on the hill. I have to go back."

"Oh, forget it," said Annie.

"I can't," said Jack. "The book doesn't belong to us. Plus my notebook's in my bag. With all my notes."

"Hurry!" said Annie.

Jack hurried down the rope ladder.

He leaped to the ground.

He raced past the Pteranodon, through the ferns, through the tall grass and up the hill.

He looked down.

There was his bag, lying on the ground. On top of it was the dinosaur book.

But now the valley below was filled with Anatosauruses. All standing guard around the nests.

Where had they been? Did fear of the

Tyrannosaurus send them home?

Jack took a deep breath.

Ready! Steady! Go!

He charged down the hill. He leaped to his rucksack. He scooped it up. He grabbed the dinosaur book.

A terrible tuba sound! Another! Another! All the Anatosauruses were bellowing at him.

Jack ran.

He raced up to the hilltop.

He started down the hill.

He stopped.

The Tyrannosaurus rex was back! And he was standing between Jack and the tree house!

8

A Giant Shadow

Jack jumped behind the magnolia tree.

His heart was beating so fast he could hardly think.

He peeped out at the giant monster. The horrible-looking creature was opening and closing his huge jaws. His teeth were as big as steak knives.

Don't panic. Think.

Jack peered down at the valley.

Good. The duck-billed dinosaurs were sticking close to their nests.

Jack looked back at the Tyrannosaurus.

Good. The
monster still didn't
seem to know he
was there.

*Don't
panic.
Think.
THINK.*
Maybe there's
information in
the book.

Jack opened the
dinosaur book. He
found Tyrannosaurus rex.
He read:

*Tyrannosaurus rex was the largest meat-
eating land animal of all time. If it were
alive today, it would eat a human in
one bite.*

Great. The book was no help at all.

OK. He couldn't hide on the other side of the hill. The Anatosauruses might stampede.

OK. He couldn't run to the tree house. The Tyrannosaurus might run faster.

OK. Maybe he should just wait. Wait for the monster to leave.

Jack peeped round the tree.

The Tyrannosaurus had wandered *closer* to the hill.

Something caught Jack's eye. Annie was coming down the rope ladder!

Was she crazy? What was she doing?

Jack watched Annie hop off the ladder. She went straight over to the Pteranodon. She was talking to him. She was flapping her arms. She pointed at Jack, at the sky, at the tree house.

She *was* crazy! "Go! Go back up the tree!" Jack whispered. "Go!" Suddenly he heard a roar.

The Tyrannosaurus rex was looking in his direction.

Jack dropped to the ground.

The Tyrannosaurus rex was coming towards the hill.

Jack felt the ground shaking.

Should he run? Crawl back into Dinosaur Valley? Climb the magnolia tree?

Just then a giant shadow covered Jack. He looked up.

The Pteranodon was gliding overhead. The giant creature sailed down towards the top of the hill.

He was coming straight for Jack.

9

The Amazing Ride

The Pteranodon coasted down to the ground.

He stared at Jack with his bright, alert eyes.

What was Jack supposed to do? Climb on? *But I'm too heavy*, thought Jack.

Don't think. Just do it.

Jack looked at the Tyrannosaurus.

He was starting up the hill. His giant teeth were flashing in the sunlight.

OK. *Don't think. Just do it!*

Jack put his book in his bag. Then he

eased down onto
the Pteranodon's back.

He held on tightly.

The creature moved forward.
He spread out his wings – and
lifted off the ground!

They teetered this way. Then that.
Jack nearly fell off.

The Pteranodon steadied himself, then
rose into the sky.

Jack looked down. The Tyrannosaurus
was chomping the air and staring up at
him.

The Pteranodon glided away.

He sailed over the hilltop.

He circled over the valley. Over all the
nests filled with babies. Over all the giant
duck-billed dinosaurs.

Then the Pteranodon soared out over
the plain – over the Triceratops, who was

grazing
in the high grass.

It was amazing! It was
a miracle!

Jack felt like a bird. As light as
a feather.

The wind was rushing through his
hair. The air smelled sweet and fresh.

He whooped. He laughed.

Jack couldn't believe it. He was riding
on the back of an ancient flying reptile!

The Pteranodon sailed over the stream,
over the ferns and bushes.

Then he carried Jack down to the base of the oak tree.

When they came to a stop, Jack slid off the creature's back. And landed on the ground.

Then the Pteranodon took off again and glided into the sky.

"Bye, Henry," whispered Jack.

"Are you OK?" Annie shouted from the tree house.

Jack pushed his glasses into place. He kept staring up at the Pteranodon.

"Jack, are you OK?" Annie called.

Jack looked up at Annie. He smiled.

"Thanks for saving my life," he said. "That was really fun."

"Climb up!" said Annie.

Jack tried to stand. His legs were wobbly.

He felt a bit dizzy.

"Hurry!" shouted Annie. "He's coming!"

Jack looked round. The Tyrannosaurus was heading straight towards him!

Jack bolted to the ladder. He grabbed the sides and started up.

"Hurry! Hurry!" screamed Annie.

Jack scrambled into the tree house.

"He's coming towards the tree!" Annie cried.

Suddenly something slammed against the oak tree.

The tree house shook like a leaf.

Jack and Annie tumbled into the books.

"Make a wish!" cried Annie.

"We need the book! The one with the picture of Frog Valley!" said Jack. "Where is it?"

He pushed some books aside. He had to find that book.

There it was!

He grabbed it and tore through it, looking for the photograph of the Frog Valley woods.

He found it! Jack pointed to the picture.

"I wish we could go home!" he shouted.

The wind began to moan. Softly at first.

"Hurry!" Jack yelled.

The wind picked up. It was whistling now.

The tree house started to spin.

It spun faster and faster.

Jack closed his eyes. He held on tightly to Annie.

Then everything was still.

Absolutely still.

10

Home Before Dark

A bird began to sing.

Jack opened his eyes. He was still pointing at the picture of the Frog Valley woods.

He peeped out of the tree-house window. Outside he saw exactly the same view.

"We're home," whispered Annie.

The woods were lit with a golden late-afternoon light. The sun was about to set.

No time had passed since they'd left.

"Ja-ack! An-nie!" a voice called from the distance.

"That's Mum," said Annie, pointing.

Jack saw their mother far away.

She was standing in front of their house. She looked very tiny.

"An-nie! Ja-ack!" she called.

Annie stuck her head out of the window and shouted, "Com-ing!"

Jack still felt dazed. He just stared at Annie.

"What happened to us?" he said.

"We took a trip in a magic tree house," said Annie simply.

"But it's the same time as when we left," said Jack.

Annie shrugged.

"And how did it take us so far away?" said Jack. "And so long ago?"

"You just looked at a book and said you wished we could go there," said Annie. "And the magic tree house took us there."

"But *how*?" said Jack. "And who built

this magic tree house? Who put all these books here?"

"A magic person, I suppose," said Annie.

A magic person?

"Oh, look," said Jack. "I almost forgot about this." He reached into his pocket and pulled out the gold medallion. "Someone lost this back there . . . in dinosaur land. Look, there's a letter M on it."

Annie's eyes were wide. "Do you think M stands for *magic person*?" she said.

"I don't know," said Jack. "I just know someone went to that place before us."

"Ja–ack! An–nie!" came the distant cry again.

Annie poked her head out of the window. "Com–ing!" she shouted.

Jack put the gold medallion back in his pocket.

He pulled the dinosaur book out of his bag. And put it back with all the other books.

Then he and Annie took one last look around the tree house.

"Goodbye, house," whispered Annie.

Jack slung his rucksack over his shoulder. He pointed at the ladder.

Annie started down. Jack followed.

Seconds later they hopped onto the ground and started walking out of the woods.

"No one's going to believe our story," said Jack.

"So let's not tell anyone," said Annie.

"Dad won't believe it," said Jack.

"He'll say it was a dream," said Annie.

"Mum won't believe it," said Jack.

"She'll say it was pretend," said Annie.

"My teacher won't believe it," said
Jack.

"She'll say you're crazy," said Annie.

"We better not tell anyone," said Jack.

"I've already said that," said Annie.

Jack sighed. "I think I'm starting to not believe it myself," he said.

They left the woods and started up the road towards their house.

As they walked past all the houses in their street, the trip to dinosaur time *did* seem more and more like a dream.

Only *this* world and *this* time seemed real.

Jack reached into his pocket. He clasped the gold medallion.

He felt the engraving of the letter M. It made his fingers tingle.

Jack laughed. Suddenly he felt very happy.

He couldn't explain what had happened today. But he knew for sure that their trip in the magic tree house had been real.

Absolutely real.

"Tomorrow," Jack said softly, "we'll go back to the woods."

"Of course," said Annie.

"And we'll climb up to the treehouse," said Jack.

"Of course," said Annie.

"And we'll see what happens next," said Jack.

"Of course," said Annie. "Race you!"

And they set off together, running for home.

Magic Tree House

CASTLE OF MYSTERY

Mary Pope Osborne

*Climb the ladder to the Magic Tree House.
There's a world of adventure inside!*

Jack and Annie are travelling
back in time again!

At first, it's all very exciting, with a
castle, a banquet and knights in shining
armour. But when they find themselves
trapped in dark, creepy dungeons, Jack
and Annie will need to come up
with a clever escape plan . . .

ISBN: 978 1 862 30524 3